Ella's Toys

I don't care,
I **WON'T** share!
Not anytime,
Not anywhere!

This is mine,
That's mine too.
All for me,
None for you.

SEE my doll?
My fancy car?
My glitter wand
With purple star?

Now go away,
Over there.
'Cause these are mine
And I won't share!

All my things
To myself,
Just for me
And no one else!

You have your toys,
All your stuff,
But maybe that's
Not enough?

Was I nice?
Did I care?
Was I kind?
Should I share?

Now I know
What to do.
For my friends
I'll come through.

Come on over,
Take a turn,
Share a toy,
Play and learn.

Yours for me,
Mine for you,
And back again
Until we're through.

All together
We can play,
Sharing toys
Every day.